PEST SIDE STORY

MW00953415

Antie

Spider Web Café

Eat in! Take out!

FRESH FROM OUR WEB TO YOUR PROBOSCIS!

Looking for a new hive?

We can help!

Queen Bee Real Estate

A Hive is a Home

CAST:

Ladybug:

Ladybug previously wrote, directed, produced, and starred in more than fifty brilliant, wonderful, Fly-free productions. She'd like to thank her little brother, Fly . . . thanks for nothing, that is!

Fly:

This is Fly's stage debut. He is very happy to be the STAR of this show, and would like to say his sister is definitely NOT the star. And now it's in writing—ha-ha-ha-ha-ha!

Also featuring:

The Monarch Butterfly Ballet Company

Spinning Spider Trapeze Artists

Spot-On Ladybird Roller Skaters and

The World-Famous Cockroach Chorus Line!

* *

For Herminio

DIAL BOOKS FOR YOUNG READERS
A division of Penguin Young Readers Group
Published by The Penguin Group
Penguin Group (USA) Inc., 375 Hudson Street, New York, NY 10014, U.S.A.
Penguin Group (Canada), 90 Eglinton Avenue East, Suite 700, Toronto, Ontario, Canada M4P 2Y3
(a division of Pearson Penguin Canada Inc.)
Penguin Books Ltd, 80 Strand, London WC2R 0RL, England
Penguin Ireland, 25 St. Stephen's Green, Dublin 2, Ireland (a division of Penguin Books Ltd)
Penguin Group (Australia), 707 Collins Street, Melbourne, Victoria 3008
(a division of Pearson Australia Group Pty Ltd)
Penguin Books India Pvt Ltd, 11 Community Centre, Panchsheel Park, New Delhi - 110 017, India
Penguin Group (NZ), 67 Apollo Drive, Rosedale, Auckland 0632, New Zealand
(a division of Pearson New Zealand Ltd)
Penguin Books, Rosebank Office Park, 181 Jan Smuts Avenue, Parktown North 2193, South Africa
Penguin China, B7 Jaiming Center, 27 East Third Ring Road North, Chaoyang District, Beijing 100020, China
Penguin Books Ltd, Registered Offices: 80 Strand, London WC2R 0RL, England

Designed by Nancy R. Leo-Kelly
Manufactured in China on acid-free paper
10 9 8 7 6 5 4 3 2 1

Library of Congress Cataloging-in-Publication Data
Jamieson, Victoria.
Pest in show / music and lyrics by Victoria Jamieson.
p. cm.
At head of title: Backyard Theater Presents
Summary: Ladybug's efforts to put on a show for her family and friends may be ruined if her little brother, Fly, gets in on the act—or maybe not.
ISBN 978-0-8037-3701-3 (hardcover)
[1. Musicals—Fiction. 2. Theater—Fiction. 3. Brothers and sisters—Fiction. 4. Humorous stories.]
I. Title. II. Title: Backyard Theater Presents.
PZ7.J1568Pes 2013   [E]—dc23 2012001410

The illustrations for this book were created using collage and acrylic paint.

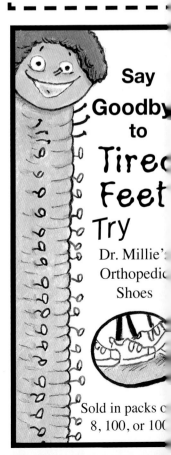

BACKYARD THEATER

Presents

PEST in SHOW

Starring

Ladybug

&

Fly

Why do you get to be first?

Music and Lyrics by Victoria Jamieson

Dial Books for Young Readers An imprint of Penguin Group (USA) Inc.

Ladybug was born
to be a star.

Her kid brother, Fly,
was born to be **a pest!**

"Can I be in your show?" he begged.

"Please?

Please?

Please?

Please?"

"Not a chance," said Ladybug.
"You are too young. You would ruin my show."

"No fair," said Fly.

Fly bugged his sister
while she rehearsed,

put on makeup,

and tried on costumes.

Finally, it was showtime!
"You sit right here, and don't move!"
said Ladybug.

The lights went down as
Ladybug began her first song.

*☆ Act 1 *☆*

Ladybug Sings
the Classics

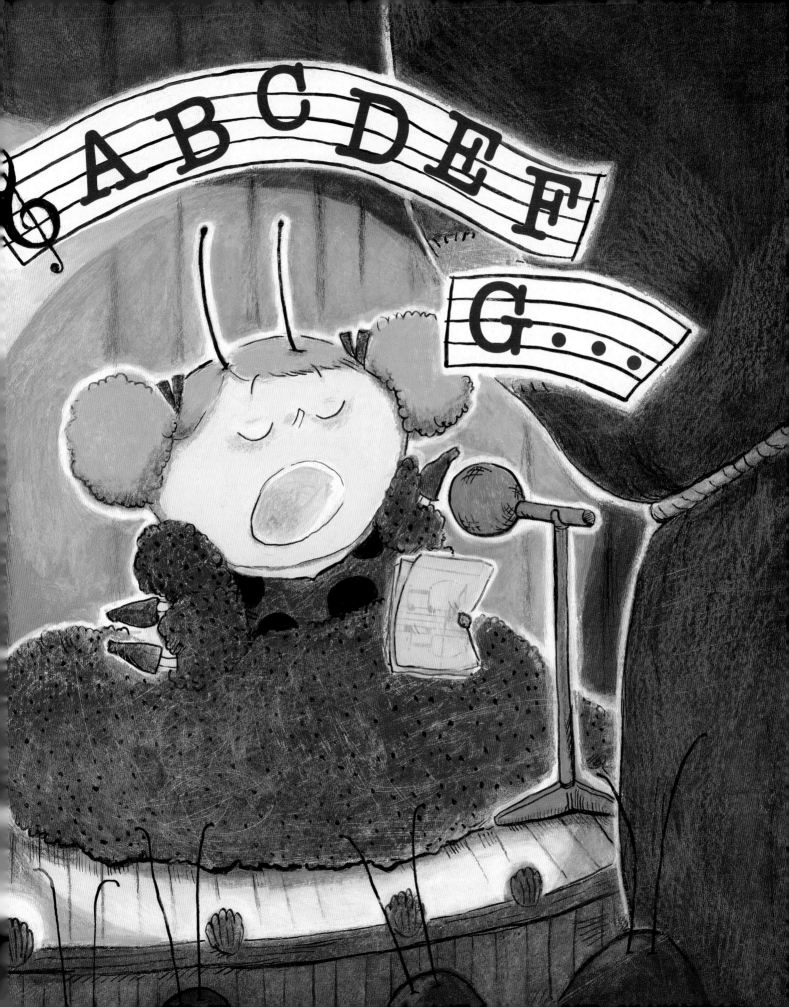

Act 1 was a wrap.

Act 2 began beautifully

until . . .

. . . the spiders dropped by.

Cut!

That was the end of Act 2.

Act 3

the beautiful! The talented!

The one you've all been waiting for...

Ladybug!

Composed by EARWIG VAN BEETHOVEN
(to the tune of "The Wheels on the Bus")

The wheels on the bugs go round and round,
Round and round,
Round and round.
The wheels on the bugs go round and round,
All through the town.

Ladybug is the best best best,
Best best best,
Best best best.
Her kid brother Fly's a pest pest pest,
All through the town.

Act 3 was
sensational!

Until . . .

. . . the pests got their revenge.

Fly gave the performance of a lifetime.
For some reason, his sister did not
appreciate it.

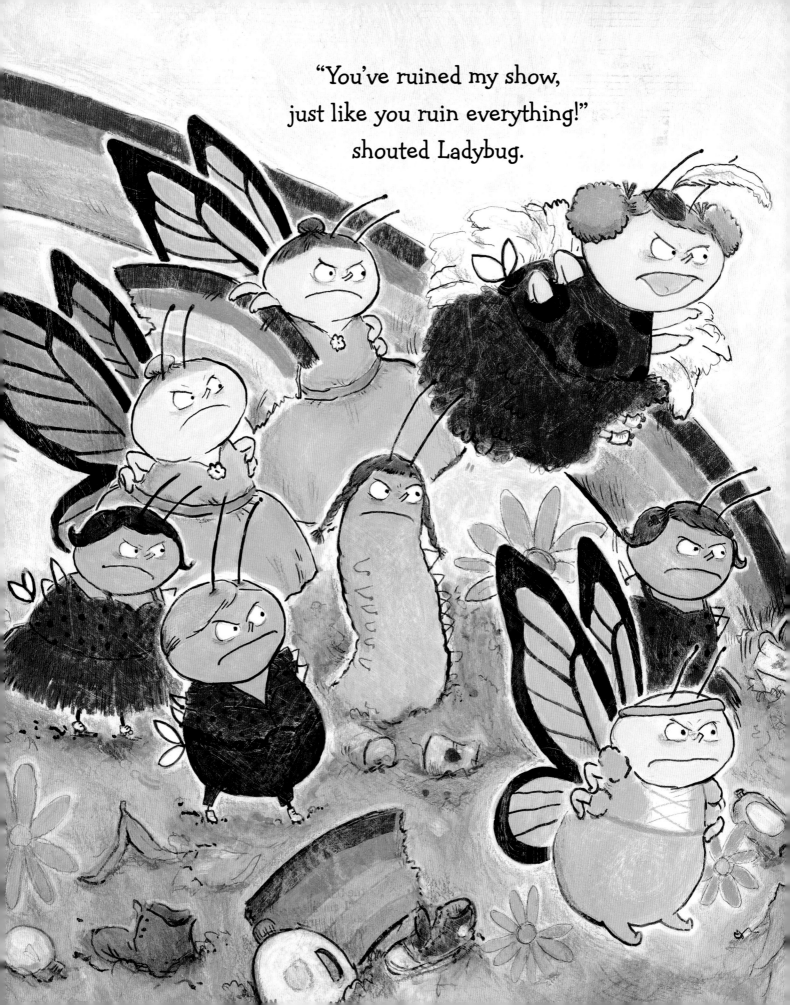

"You've ruined my show,
just like you ruin everything!"
shouted Ladybug.

"You never gave me a chance.
You never let me do anything with you!"
yelled Fly.

Ladybug glared at Fly.
Fly glared right back.
Clearly, there was only one thing to do.

Grand Finale

All-bug,
winner-take-all

Dance-Off!

Music and Lyrics by THE BEETLES
(to the tune of "Do Your Ears Hang Low")

Can you dance the bug?
Can you shimmy? Cut a rug?

Let me see you flap your wing.
Let me see you shake your sting.

Let me see you stomp your feet
Like you're on decaying meat.

Can you dance the bug?

Can you buzz? Can you fly?
Do you have a compound eye?

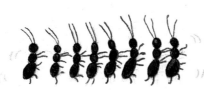

Can you wiggle like a worm?
Can you squiggle like a germ?

Can you jump to six-foot-three?
Not unless you are a flea!

Come and dance the bug!

"HILARIOUS!"
—Cousin Ralph

SIX THUMBS UP!"
—Roger Fleabert

"I'D PAY A QUARTER
TO SEE THIS SHOW."
—Aunt Mildred

The show was a smash hit!
After all, Ladybug was born to
be a star.

And maybe, just maybe,
her brother was born to be . . .

. . . her co-star.

"I still think my name should
be first," said Fly.
"Dream on," said Ladybug.

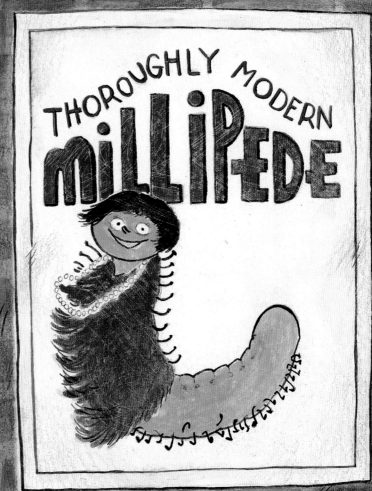